Muslim Child

a collection of short stories and poems
by

RUKHSANA KHAN

illustrations by
PATTY GALLINGER

sidebars by
IRFAN ALLI

Napoleon Publishing

Irfan Alli may be contacted at irfanalli@idirect.ca
You may visit Rukhsana Khan's website at www.rukhsanakhan.com

Napoleon Publishing gratefully acknowledges the support of the Canada Council for the Arts for our publishing program.

Le Conseil des Arts du Canada | The Canada Council for the Arts

Napoleon Publishing/RendezVous Press
Toronto, Ontario, Canada
1-877-730-9052

First hardcover edition printed by Napoleon Publishing in 1999 (0-929141-61-X)

Printed in Canada

09 08 07 06 05   6 5 4 3 2

National Library of Canada Cataloguing in Publication Data

Khan, Rukhsana
    Muslim child : a collection of short stories and poems

ISBN 0-929141-61-X (bound).—ISBN 0-929141-96-2 (pbk.)

1. Muslim children—Literary collections. 2. Muslims—Social life and customs—Literary collections. I. Gallinger, Patty II. Title.

PS8571.H42M87 1999   jC818'.5409   C99-930231-0
PZ7.K52653Mu 1999

TABLE OF CONTENTS

MUSLIM CHILD

by Rukhsana Khan

Muslim Child
Child of Peace
Child of War
From a far-off distant shore
What do your black eyes see?

My eyes are not only black.
Sometimes they are blue as the sky
Or green as the tropical sea
Or brown as the trunk of a palm tree
And every shade in between.

My skin can be black as molasses
Or as pink as the blush on a rose
As golden as freshly made honey
Or dark copper brown as a penny
And every shade in between.

I am the richest of the rich
And the poorest of the poor
As famous as famous can be;
A general's child, pampered and bored
A soldier's child, orphaned by war
And every rank in between.

I come from many countries
Speaking many languages
But with one set of beliefs.
I believe in Noah and Jesus and Abraham
Muhammad and Moses and in God who sent them
And in every messenger in between.
(God bless them.)

So then,
Muslim Child
Child of Peace
What do your bright eyes see?

I see that we're each a piece in
the puzzle of humanity.
I'll try to understand you
If you'll try to understand me.

SURAH AL-FATIHA
(THE OPENING)
Chapter One of the Quran

1.

In the Name of God the Most Beneficent,
the Most Merciful.

2.

All praise is due to God alone, the Sustainer
of all the worlds (All realms of existence).

3.

The Most Beneficent, the Most Merciful.

4.

Lord of the Day of Judgement.

5.

Thee alone do we worship; and unto Thee
alone do we turn for help.

6.

Guide us to the straight way.

7.

The way of those upon whom You have bestowed
Your blessings, not of those who have been
condemned, nor of those who go astray.

FAJR

(CANADA)

"Wake up, lazybones!" Jamal sat up and rubbed his eyes. His sister Seema stood in the doorway. "Didn't you hear *Abi* calling? It's time for *Fajr*."

Jamal glanced at the clock. Four-thirty in the morning.

As soon as Seema was gone, Jamal flopped back down. The mattress hugged his tired body, massaging his aching muscles. He felt so cozy. He wished he could bring the sink to his bed, make *wudu* and pray lying down.

"Jamal," his father called, "are you up?"

Jamal bolted upright. "Yes, Abi."

Pulling back the covers, he swung his legs over the side of the bed. He took a deep stretch as a yawn passed through him. The pillow beckoned. He ignored it and tested the bare wood of the floor with his big toe. Snatching it back, he shivered.

He should just get up. The sooner he prayed, the sooner he could go back to sleep.

Seema was back. "Get up right now, or I'm telling."

"Okay, okay. I'm up," he muttered under his

Abi: Arabic word for "my father"

Fajr: first prayer of the five daily prayers. It is offered before sunrise.

wudu: washing performed before prayer

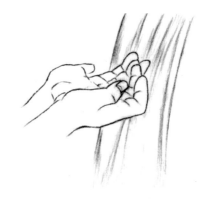

7

breath. "It's so hard being *Muslim*."

Seema heard him. "I'm telling! You don't want to be Muslim!"

"I didn't say that! I just said it's hard, you know, getting up in the middle of the night to pray."

Seema sneered at him. "Don't you know that prayer is a gift? God doesn't need your prayer, you do." With that, she left again.

Muslim: a Muslim follows the way of life called Islam. More than one-fifth of the world's people are Muslims.

If that were true, thought Jamal, why didn't he feel any better after he prayed? Was there something wrong with him?

Jamal made his way to the bathroom. Turning on the light, he staggered as it pierced his eyes. Groping around till he could see without squinting, he looked at the toilet. Naw! He didn't have to go. It would waste too much time.

Seema poked her head through the doorway. Too late he wished he'd shut the door. "And don't forget to make wudu properly. Remember, prayer is the key to paradise, and wudu is the key to prayer."

"Yeah, yeah. Get lost."

Seema turned red. "I'm telling Abi. . ."

"Okay, sorry. Now let me make wudu."

Seema started to say something, but changed her mind and left.

Jamal began wudu. He washed his hands three times. Rinsed his mouth three times. Cleaned his nostrils three times and washed his face three times and his arms up to the elbows, three times. Wetting his hands, he passed them over his hair and cleaned his ears, inside, outside and behind them.

Finally he heaved his right foot into the sink and washed between his toes and up to his ankle three times. Then he did his left foot.

Now he was ready to pray. He dried himself as best he could and went down to the living room. Seema was already praying her *sunnah*.

Standing solemnly on his prayer mat, he raised his hands to his ears and said, "*Allahu Akbar*. God is Great." Then he crossed his arms over his chest.

Jamal kept his eyes down, reciting the Quranic verses carefully. The two sunnah *rakaats* went quickly. His sister had finished her prayers and was quietly saying her *dhikr*, her praise, the beads on her *tasbih* clicking as she counted them off.

Jamal began his *fard*, the more important prayer. He was halfway through when he had a big problem. He had to fart.

He couldn't concentrate anymore. He simply said the words as fast as he could, without even trying to mean them.

He should break his prayer. He should make a fresh wudu, but he only had one rakaat left! Maybe he could hang in there. He squeezed and hoped nothing would slip out.

He finished standing and went into *ruku*. This was worse. It was harder to squeeze. He quickly stood back up, said "*Sami Allah hu liman hamida...* God has heard the one who praises Him," and went down for *sujud*.

His nose and forehead were pressed to the prayer mat, but his mind was elsewhere. He twitched from side to side.

He was sitting now. And it was a little easier. But down he went again in *sujud*.

sunnah: additional prayers prayed by Prophet Muhammad (peace be upon him)

rakaat: a unit of prayer

dhikr: remembrance of God through praise, e.g. "God is the Greatest."

tasbih: a string of beads, similar to a rosary, used for counting dhikr

fard: obligatory prayer

sujud: the name for the prostrating position of prayer

9

ruku: the name for the bowing position of prayer

sujud: the name for the prostrating position of prayer

jalsa: the name for the sitting position of prayer

ashhadu: a part of the prayer where the right forefinger is raised to testify that there is nothing worthy of worship but God and that Muhammad (peace be upon him) is the prophet of God.

Swaying side to side, he desperately tried to contain himself.

With relief he sat back up, in *jalsa*. He was almost there. Just a few more words, and he'd be done.

He pressed his weight down on his foot, saying the words so fast they were a blur on his tongue. He shifted from one foot to the other. A few more seconds and he'd be clear. He had just raised his right forefinger for the *ashhadu* when it happened.

No more need to squeeze. No more need to rush. His prayer was ruined. But it was so quiet and so small. Maybe it didn't count. And maybe Seema hadn't heard. He finished his prayer as if nothing had happened. Then picked up his prayer mat.

"Wait a minute," cried Seema.

"What?"

"I heard you."

"What?" said Jamal innocently.

"You're so gross. Go make wudu and pray all over again."

Jamal dragged himself back to the bathroom. He turned the water on but didn't make wudu. Darned if he'd pray again. The thought made him pause. Naw! Would he go to hell just for missing one little prayer? Would he? Naw!

After what he thought was long enough, he shut off the tap and peaked up and down the hallway. No Seema. He tiptoed to her bedroom, listening at the door. She was snoring. Further down the hall, he could hear the deeper snoring of his father. They were asleep.

He tiptoed back to his bed and flopped down pulling up the covers. Letting his mind go blank, he waited for sleep to come. After a while his foot was itchy. He rubbed it against the scratchy blanket and rolled over onto his stomach. Again he let his mind go blank and waited.

10

Nothing. Bending his knee, he lifted his foot and let it fall. Thunk. He did it again. Thunk. And again. Thunk.

After the hundredth "Thunk", he gave up, rolled over and fixed his sheets. He closed his eyes, trying hard to relax. Now his back was itchy. Turning on his side to scratch it, he saw the clock.

"Five o'clock!" he groaned, rolling over again. If he'd made wudu and prayed again, he would have been asleep by now. He pushed the thought away and started to breathe slowly and deeply. He thought of nothing but soft blackness and relaxed every muscle in his body.

What was that noise? He'd been hearing it for some time, but now it was getting louder. What was it? It was coming from outside. He should have known. The sound of birds singing. Every stupid bird in the neighborhood was rejoicing in the coming sunrise.

Abi would say they were singing *Allah's* praise. Praying Fajr in their own way.

Jamal squeezed his eyes shut and blocked his ears. He continued his deep breathing and forced his body to relax. He stayed that way for a long time. Finally he rolled over and glanced at the clock again.

"Five-thirty!" He might as well get up and pray. He sure wasn't going to get any rest until he did.

Water dripping from a fresh wudu, he stood once again on his prayer mat and lifted his hands to his ears. "*Allahu Akbar.* God is Great."

This time he prayed slowly. It was easier to concentrate. He said his *salaams* at the end of the prayer and picked up the tasbih to do his dhikr.

"*Alhamdulillah*, all praise is for God, *Alhamdulillah*..."

Allah: Allah is the Arabic word for God. Muslims worship the same God that the Jews and Christians worship. Mulsims believe that God is One and Jesus (peace be upon him) is a prophet of God.

salaams: a statement of peace at the end of the prayer. "Unto you be peace and the mercy of God." This is said turning to the right and to the left.

How peaceful it is, he thought as his lips said the dhikr and his fingers counted off the beads.

He was done. But instead of going back to bed, he went to the window.

The trees hid the horizon, but he could see the rosy glow in the east. The dew on the grass sparkled faintly through the morning mist. He opened the window and smelled the freshness of a new day. Grabbing a quilt, he went outside. The dew was cold where it sprinkled his feet through the straps of his sandals.

He sat on the porch in a rocking chair and watched the sunrise.

That's where his father found him, a few hours later, asleep with a *Quran* in his hands.

Quran: Muslim holy book. Muslims believe that it is God's last revelation to mankind. It was revealed to the Prophet Muhammad (peace be upon him) and is a source of guidance and healing.

SAYINGS OF
PROPHET MUHAMMAD
(Peace be upon him)

Kindness is a mark of faith
and whoever is not kind
has no faith.

God does not look at your appearance
or your possessions,
but He looks at your heart
and the things you do.

THE BLACK GHOST
(CANADA)

"*Assalaamu alaikum*," called Nabeel, as he rushed out the door.

"Wait," said his mother, putting on her *hijaab*, then letting down her *niqaab* so it hung over her face.

Nabeel peeked up and down the road. It was safe. No one was watching.

She tousled his hair, saying, "Your first day at a new school. Are you nervous?"

He shook his head quickly. Why didn't she hurry? Someone might see her. He felt a quick kiss through the niqaab, the black cloth covering her face, then he raced down the steps. The sooner he was gone, the sooner she'd go back inside, where no one could see her.

"Have fun," she called.

Nabeel nodded and turned the corner. Out of nowhere a boy crashed into him.

Pencils, erasers and paper went flying. "Sorry. Are you okay? It was my fault. I should look where

Assalaamu alaikum: a Muslim greeting, meaning "Peace be with you."
"Wa alaikum assalaam" is the reply, meaning "And on you be peace too."

hijaab: the head covering worn by Muslim women. Some Muslim women choose to go further, also covering their faces.

niqaab: the word commonly used for the face-covering that many Muslim women wear

women's dress: There is no real "Muslim" cultural dress. Any clothes, from any culture, can be adapted to fit Islamic dress codes as long as they cover the woman fully, are not transparent and are loose-fitting.

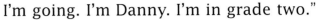

I'm going. I'm Danny. I'm in grade two."

Danny helped Nabeel up. They picked up their things and started walking together. It turned out they were in the same class. By recess, they were best friends, but in the back of his mind, Nabeel worried. What if Danny saw his mother? Would he still be his friend?

A few days later, Nabeel's mother followed him out the door. "Where are you going?" he asked.

"Shopping and to the library, if that's okay with you."

Nabeel tried to walk ahead, but his mother kept pace. Nabeel tried running. His mother jogged along beside him, easily. When they got to the spot where he usually met Danny, Nabeel was worried. Danny was late. Nabeel was glad. Finally, his mother turned back. Nabeel gave a little wave none of the other kids would notice.

Footsteps pounded on the sidewalk behind him. It was Danny. His face was white and his eyes were wild. He grabbed Nabeel's hand and dragged him the rest of the way to school.

"What is it?" Nabeel cried, trying to free his hand. But Danny didn't stop to explain.

The bell had rung and they burst into the classroom.

The teacher said, "What's the matter Danny? Were you climbing trees again? Did you fall down?"

"No," gasped Danny. "I saw a ghost!"

"A ghost?" cried the kids in the class.

"A big black ghost!" said Danny. "It floated down the sidewalk after me. All I could see were its hands and slits where the eyes should be!" Danny shivered.

Nabeel came forward and put a hand on Danny's shoulder. "It wasn't a ghost."

"How do you know?" asked a girl.

Nabeel grew red. "Um, I mean, it couldn't be a ghost. Not in the middle of the day. Maybe it was just a person dressed up."

16

Danny shook his head. "What kind of person wears clothes like that?"

Nabeel shrugged. "Some people do. Not everyone dresses like us."

"That's right," said the teacher. "Now, get to your seats. Class is about to begin."

Nabeel sighed with relief. A few more questions and everyone would have known his secret.

On the way home, Danny asked Nabeel, "How come we never play at your house?"

Nabeel didn't know what to say.

"Well?" asked Danny. "When can I come over?"

Nabeel shrugged. "Um, let's play hide-and-seek."

Danny kicked a stone out of his way. "We've got to get home for lunch."

"I'll be it."

"Okay."

Nabeel counted to twenty and then went searching. He looked behind the fence, in some bushes, under a bench, and beneath the slide. He couldn't find Danny anywhere. Finally he cupped his hands to his mouth and called, "I give up. Where are you?"

He heard laughter above him. Danny was very high up, half-hidden by the leaves.

"Very funny, Danny. Come down, now. It's getting late."

Danny stopped laughing. His face looked pale and pinched.

Nabeel cupped his hands around his mouth. "Come on. You'll be late for lunch."

Danny's voice was shaky. "I can't."

"You climbed up. So climb down. Come on."

Danny gripped the trunk of the tree and shook his head. He had to go down. Nabeel would think he was silly. But he couldn't.

"I'll go get help," said Nabeel.

"No! Don't leave me!"

men's dress: Like women, Muslim men are also required to dress modestly in loose-fitting, non transparent clothing. There are also restrictions on what they are allowed to reveal. At the very least, a man is required to cover between his navel and his knee. This includes the times he is at home with his family, as well as in public, at places like swimming pools.

Nabeel looked around the park. It was deserted. Everyone was home having lunch. What could he do? "I have to get help," he insisted.

"Don't go!"

"I'll be right back."

"No!" Nabeel heard a loud crack, and the branch Danny had been sitting on broke. Danny screamed and grabbed onto another branch, desperately holding on.

"Help," cried Danny.

"Don't let go," said Nabeel. "I'll get the teacher."

"No! I'll fall!" Nabeel was about to go anyway, when Danny cried even louder. "The ghost! Run, Nabeel!"

Nabeel was so relieved. He ran right up to his mother. Without wasting a breath, she ran to the foot of the tree and began to climb.

Danny shifted, trying to grab better hold of the trunk when he heard a creak. The branch plunged, hanging at a bad angle. His hands were slipping. They were tired. "I can't hold on anymore!" he screamed. Then suddenly he didn't have to.

An arm dressed in black circled his waist and set him firmly on top of a thick, strong branch. He hugged the tree trunk and stared at the Black Ghost, sitting a branch away.

"I'll just set you there a minute. Phew! I need a rest," Danny heard her say.

Nabeel took a deep breath and called, "It's okay, Danny, she's my mom."

Danny said, "Your mom's a ghost?!"

Nabeel's mother laughed. "It's a good thing I'm not. A ghost couldn't have picked you up. You're heavy."

Danny was silent. He didn't want to look at the slits where the eyes should be.

"Are you ready to go down now?" asked Nabeel's mother.

There was no other way. Danny plucked up his courage and looked at her again. This time he saw

children's dress: the Islamic restrictions for men's and women's dress are not absolutely required of children, although as they get closer to puberty, children are encouraged more and more to dress like Muslim adults. That way they are accustomed to it by the time the Islamic dress code is required of them.

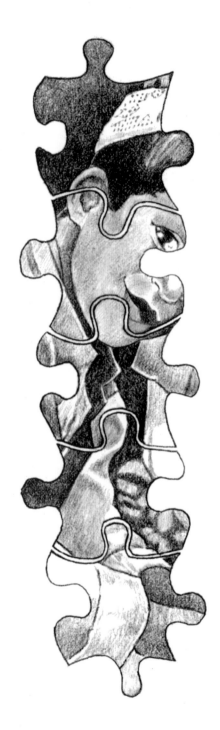

inside the slits. He saw two pretty black eyes. They were smiling. And she didn't sound scary. "You want me to carry you down or not?"

Silently, Danny nodded.

Danny shut his eyes tight and clung to the lady in black. She smelled a little like his own mother. Like soap.

He felt the two of them moving down, slowly, inch by inch, until they stopped. When he opened his eyes, they were safe on the ground.

The lady knelt and paused. Waiting. "You can let go now, Danny."

Danny quickly slid off her knee. "Oops. Sorry."

"That's okay." She checked his arms and legs. "You've been shaken up a bit. Are you all right?"

Danny nodded, his face red. Nabeel must think he was silly for climbing so high. He must think he was a coward for being scared. Who'd want to be friends with a coward? Not me, thought Danny. Quietly, he turned to go home.

The lady called, "Can we walk you home?"

"Oh, no," said Danny, still a little afraid.

"Wait," she said, fishing in the pocket of her black dress. "How about a lollipop? It's great for the shakes."

Danny smiled. "Oh, yes, please."

She said, "Are you sure you wouldn't like us to walk you home?"

"Okay," said Danny.

Danny and Nabeel skipped along, followed by the black ghost. Nabeel was relieved. "Are you still my friend?"

Danny nodded. "If you're still mine."

Nabeel grinned.

With his mouth full of lollipop, Danny whispered, "Why didn't you tell me you had such a nice mom?"

Nabeel smiled. It was nice not to have a secret any more.

PROPHETS

Muslims believe that prophets are men whom God chose to guide the rest of mankind. The Quran mentions twenty-five by name, but also says that God sent prophets to every nation of the world. Their role was to guide and teach their people.

Muslims believe that Islam started with the prophet Adam (peace be upon him) and evolved from one prophet to another, with prophet Muhammad (peace be upon him) being the last prophet. This means that all the prophets invited their people to believe in the same God, and to be "Muslim" (one who attains peace through submission to the will of God). One of the pillars of faith for Muslims is to believe in all the prophets.

Some prophets also received revelations. Muslims believe in the original divine books revealed to them. Muslims have respect and reverence for all of the prophets and take them as role models. Below are the names of the twenty-five prophets mentioned in the Quran.

Adam
Idris (*Enoch*)
Nuh (*Noah*)
Hud (*Heber*)
Salih (*Methusaleh*)
Lut (*Lot*)
Ibrahim (*Abraham*)
Ismail (*Ishmael*)
Ishaq (*Isaac*)
Yaqub (*Jacob*)
Yusuf (*Joseph*)
Shu'aib (*Jethro*)
Ayyub (*Job*)
Dhulkifl (*Ezekiel*)

Musa (*Moses*)
Harun (*Aaron*)
Dawud (*David*)
Sulayman (*Solomon*)
Ilias (*Elias*)
Alyasa (*Elisha*)
Yunus (*Jonah*)
Zakariya (*Zachariah*)
Yahya (*John the Baptist*)
Isa (*Jesus*)
Muhammad

Peace be upon them all.

A SAYING OF
PROPHET MUHAMMAD

(Peace be upon him)

Islam is built on five pillars:
testifying there is no god but God and
that Muhammad is the messenger of God,
performing the prayers,
paying the zakaat,
making the pilgrimage to Mecca,
and fasting in Ramadan.

AZEEZA'S FIRST FAST

(UNITED STATES)

Azeeza and her father climbed all the way to the roof of their apartment building. They came up twice a year, at the beginning and end of the month of *Ramadan.*

If the *new moon* was to be seen, it would be right above the glowing spot where the sun was disappearing.

Azeeza saw it first, a thin curved line in the rosy brightness of the sky. Like angels had taken a piece of white chalk and drawn a "C", only backwards.

Azeeza pointed. "Look father. *Ramadan Mubarak*! Tomorrow we will fast."

Her father smiled. "You're too young. Maybe next year."

"I can do it."

"It's a long time to go without eating or drinking. And you have to wake up early."

"I can do it. I might even fast every day like you."

"We'll see."

When they went back down to their apartment, Azeeza's mother was waiting. Azeeza said, "We're fasting tomorrow, *Ummi.* It's Ramadan!"

"Let her try," said her father.

Azeeza's mother looked doubtful, but agreed.

Ramadan: the Muslim month of fasting, the ninth month of the Muslim calendar

new moon: the Muslim calendar follows the lunar cycle. A new month starts every time the new moon is seen. Like the Christian calendar, the Muslim calendar has twelve months.

Ramadan Mubarak: a greeting which means "The blessings of Ramadan be with you."

Ummi: the Arabic word for "my mother"

Suhoor: the early morning meal taken before dawn when fasting

Muslims must pray to God five times each day as follows:
Fajr – at dawn
Zuhr – shortly after midday
Asr – in mid-afternoon
Maghrib – right after sunset
Isha – before going to sleep

That night Azeeza went to bed early, but it was hard to sleep. She'd show them. Before she knew it, someone was shaking her shoulder. It was still dark. She was still tired. "Go away," she muttered. "I want to sleep."

Her father bent down and whispered, his warm breath tickling Azeeza's ear. "If you want to fast, you have to wake up for *Suhoor*."

Azeeza's eyes flew open. She jumped out of bed and ran to the kitchen. Her mother was setting the table. "Come and eat," she said.

Azeeza looked at the food on the table and yawned. "I'm not hungry."

Her father picked her up and set her on the chair. "You'll need your strength."

Azeeza had a banana and half a bowl of cereal. Her mother frowned, looking worried. "Eat some more. You'll get hungry."

Azeeza wrinkled her nose.

"Fine then, drink some hot chocolate. But hurry. It's almost time to stop eating."

Azeeza was finishing the last dregs of chocolate in the bottom of the cup when her father glanced at the clock and said, "It's time to start fasting."

Then they went to pray *Fajr*. During the prayer Azeeza yawned eight times. Afterward, her father kissed her and sent her back to bed.

When she woke up again, she changed her clothes, brushed her teeth (making sure not to swallow anything) and was off to school. This fasting was easy, she thought. It sure saved time.

At recess, she grinned while walking past the line at the water fountain. After recess, her mouth was a little dry, but she felt okay.

But during math, her stomach growled so loudly that the whole class heard.

"What was that?" cried Tony.

Azeeza wriggled in her seat. Were you supposed to say "excuse me" if your stomach growled?

When it was lunchtime, she walked slowly home.

She felt tired, and her stomach kept reminding her how empty it was.

Her mother met her at the door. "How is your fast?"

"Okay, I guess."

"Lie down. It's good to rest when you're fasting."

Dropping her jacket, Azeeza went to the sofa. That's when she saw the jelly bean on the floor. Red, her favourite. Before she knew it, she'd popped it into her mouth. Mmm. Sweet and juicy. After she had swallowed, she remembered she was fasting.

"Oh no!"

Her mother came running. "What's the matter? Are you all right?"

"It was an accident. I didn't mean to. Honest. I forgot. I found a jelly bean..."

Her mother was smiling. "That's okay, dear. You haven't broken your fast."

"But I ate it."

"It's okay if you forget and eat something. *Allah* was the one who gave you the food anyway. But you have to stop eating when you remember. Did you do that?"

Allah: Allah is the Arabic word for God. Muslims worship the same God that the Jews and Christians worship. Muslims believe that God is One and Jesus (peace be upon him) is a prophet of God.

Azeeza nodded.

"Just try to remember next time, okay?"

"Okay." She lay down on the sofa and dozed off. When she woke up, she felt a little thirsty but much better.

After she had prayed *Zuhr* she ran off to school.

Zuhr: the prayer shortly after midday

But that afternoon there was a problem. Tony's mother brought in a chocolate birthday cake with sprinkles, to share with the class.

"Don't you want any?" asked the teacher.

Azeeza didn't answer.

Tony said, "It's okay. She didn't put any *pig stuff* in it. I told her you can't eat pig stuff."

pig stuff: Muslims are not allowed to eat any food that contains a product from pigs.

"It's not that, " said Azeeza. "I'm fasting."

"What's that?"

She told the class.

Tony said, "Go ahead and eat it. I won't tell.

Neither will anyone else. Right?"

"Right," said the others.

Azeeza shook her head quickly. "Oh, no. I couldn't."

"Why not?" asked one girl.

"Aren't you hungry?" asked another.

"Yes."

"Then eat it."

Azeeza looked down. "I just can't."

The teacher said, "I have an idea. I'll wrap up your piece. Take it home and have it when you're finished fasting."

"Oh, yes," cried Azeeza. "Thanks, Tony."

Azeeza tucked the cake in her coat pocket. She wanted to take a lick of the chocolate icing, but she didn't. She even wished she could forget she was fasting, just for a moment, long enough to take a bite, but she didn't.

At recess, she played dodgeball. When she came in, she was so thirsty she raced to the water fountain. She took a big mouthful of ice cold water but remembered and spit it out. Her throat was still dry. She turned and marched into the classroom, looking back only once.

But by 4:00, as she trudged home tired and thirsty and hungry, she knew she couldn't make it. She didn't want to fast anymore. She had to eat. She had to drink. She wanted to eat the piece of cake in her pocket. She told her mother this as she helped her off with her coat.

"But it's not very long now. Only an hour and a half left."

Azeeza slipped to the floor. "But that's so long. I can't wait."

Her mother led her to the sofa. "You've fasted all day, it's a shame to quit now. Let's pray *Asr* and then you can rest. Read a book. The time will go by before you know it."

After they had prayed Asr, Azeeza flopped down on the sofa. She didn't feel like reading. She felt

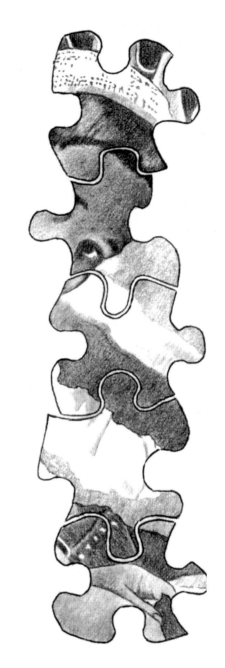

Asr: the prayer in mid-afternoon

like eating. Picking up a book, she got as far as the goodies Little Red Riding Hood was taking to Grandma's house when she remembered how hungry she was and threw the book down. Still an hour and fifteen minutes to go. Azeeza turned on the TV. There was a commercial for ice cream, then one for cereal and one for hamburgers. She shut off the TV.

Her stomach growled even louder.

In the kitchen, her mother was making pizza. The smell made Azeeza's mouth water.

Her mother looked up, "I made it especially for you."

Azeeza smiled weakly. "I can't wait."

"You're almost there."

"It's so hard. Why do they call it fasting when it goes so slow?"

Her mother laughed. "It's just the name for it, dear."

"Why do we have to fast anyway?"

"It makes you feel lucky."

Azeeza grumbled, "I don't feel lucky."

"Oh, but you are. When you've finished fasting, you can eat. Some poor people can't."

Azeeza was quiet, watching her mother put the pizza in the oven.

Her father came in. "Are you still fasting?"

Azeeza nodded.

Her father gave her a big hug. "I'm proud of you. You're such a big girl."

Yes, she was. A little girl couldn't have fasted the whole day.

"Go wash up. It's almost time to break the fast."

Azeeza ran and washed her hands.

Her mother called, "It's time."

Azeeza grabbed her piece of cake from her coat pocket and galloped for the table.

"Slow down," her mother cried. "Don't eat too fast. You'll get sick."

The sky was getting dark. They said the *dua*.

dua: a small prayer. Muslims do this by raising their hands.

28

They said: "O God, I believe in you and have fasted for Your sake. I put my trust in You. And I break my fast with food You gave me."

Azeeza took a bite of a date. It was sweet and chewy and delicious. Then she took a bite of cake. It was also sweet and chewy and delicious. She drank a big glass of water and thought she'd never tasted anything as good.

Then they went to pray *Maghrib*. Azeeza couldn't wait till they were done and could eat supper.

When the pizza came, she thought she could eat the whole thing by herself. But after two pieces she was full.

Her father said, "So, should I wake you up to fast tomorrow?"

Azeeza thought for a moment. "Maybe not tomorrow, but the next day for sure."

Azeeza fasted for four whole days over the month of Ramadan. Her dad fasted all of them, and her mother did most of them. Before she knew it, twenty-nine days had gone by, and they were climbing the stairs of the apartment building again, all the way to the roof.

If the *new moon* was to be seen, it would be right above the glowing spot where the sun was disappearing.

Azeeza saw it first, a thin curved line in the rosy brightness of the sky. Like angels had taken a piece of white chalk and drawn a "C", only backwards.

Azeeza pointed. "Look, fasting is finished. Tomorrow is *Eid-ul-Fitr. Eid Mubarak!*"

Maghrib: the prayer just after sunset

new moon: some think that the moon and star is a symbol of Islam, the way the cross is a symbol of Christianity. However, the moon and star are just symbols that some countries have adopted. The new moon is important in Islam because it determines the start of a new month and the timings of Islamic festivals. The lunar year is also about ten days shorter than the solar year. This results in Ramadan and Eid occuring in different seasons as the years pass.

Eid-ul-Fitr: Festival of Charity, called Eid for short. It is the first day of Shawwal, the month after Ramadan, and the celebration that marks the end of Ramadan. It is called the Festival of Charity because the parents must pay a "Fitr" or a charity for each person in the house, even the babies. The Fitr is equal to enough money to feed a poor person a proper meal.

Eid Mubarak: the greeting for Eid. It means "The Joys of Eid be with you."

THANK YOU, ALLAH
by Rukhsana Khan

Thank you, Allah, for the sun so bright
That shines from up above.
Thank you, Allah, for my family
Who taught me how to love.
Thank you, Allah, for the trees that give
Fruit and wood and shade.
Thank you, Allah, for the good you put
In everything you made.

For the water falling down as rain
From the cloudy sky;
For the moonbeams and the stars so bright
Shining through the night;
For the mountains standing big and tall;
The oceans deep and wide;
For the creatures that are both big and small
That run and swim and fly.

There's so much to be thankful for
So much the words can't say.
So thank you, Allah, for the many gifts
You give to me each day.

I LOVE EID
(CANADA)

I love *Eid*. Especially *Eid-ul-Fitr*. I just love Eid. We wake early and take our baths, washing till we're squeaky clean. Then we put on new clothes, our best clothes. The house is a frenzy—Dad can't find his missing sock, and Mom is doing some last minute ironing.

Samia for breakfast. Mmmm. Love those creamy noodles and bits of almonds.

No school. Ha, ha. It's too special a day. Mom and Dad take off work, too. We hug each other and wish each other "*Eid Mubarak*!" Giggling. Laughing. Smiling. Even the baby. He tries to say it, too.

Then we pack into the car, and we're on our way. I try not to get my new dress wrinkled.

We don't go to the *mosque* to pray. Oh no. It wouldn't be big enough. Everyone comes to pray on Eid, so we need a big hall.

The parking lot is packed. People of all colours, brown, white, beige and black, get out of their shiny cars and head for the prayer hall. So many colours of *Muslims*. All coming to thank God for a wonderful *Ramadan*. Women wear bright colours like red and yellow and gold. Bright as autumn leaves. With lots of glitter and sparkle. They look look like birds, tropical birds. The men look

Eid-ul-Fitr: Festival of Charity, called Eid for short. It's celebration marks the end of Ramadan.

samia: vermicelli noodles cooked in milk and sugar

Eid Mubarak: the greeting for Eid. It means "The blessings of Eid be with you."

mosque: the place where Muslims normally gather to worship together. Another common word used to mean the same thing is Masjid.

Muslim: a Muslim follows the way of life called Islam. More than one fifth of the world's people are Muslims.

Ramadan: the Muslim month of fasting

Allahu akbar: a phrase commonly said by Muslims. It means "God is the Greatest".

Imam: the spiritual leader of a Muslim community, and the leader of the prayer. He stands in front of the congregation when leading the prayer.

Straighten the lines: Muslims pray in straight lines, standing shoulder to shoulder. The men are separate from the women.

khutba: a speech or sermon

Muslim: a common mistake is to refer to Muslims as "Moslems". To call a Muslim a Moslem is actually an insult, as the two words mean two different things in the Arabic language.

The word "Moslem" has its origin in the Arabic word Zulm. The word Zulm means "to be unfair or unjust." To call someone a Moslem would therefore mean that person is unfair or unjust. The correct pronunciation is MUSLIM, and the religion is ISLAM.

The word Islam has its origin in the Arabic word Salam, which means "peace". In a religious sense, Islam means to seek to live in peace with God and His creation. This comes by following God's prescribed way of life, Islam. A person who chooses to seek this peace and follows the path of Islam is called a Muslim.

dignified, wearing turbans and robes, their beards combed neatly. And the boys have caps, little kufis, on their heads.

Inside, there is a jumble of people. Thousands and thousands, chanting "*Allahu akbar,*" and other good things.

The hall is full. It is time to pray. The *Imam* tells us to stand shoulder to shoulder. *Straighten the lines*, fill the gaps, stand together before God. Rich and poor and in-between, stand together, leave no space. God will be pleased.

The *Imam* has a microphone so we can hear. He says "Allahu Akbar" and the prayer begins. Again and again he says "Allahu akbar," raising his hands to his ears. We follow behind, the whole congregation, repeating after him. This is a special prayer, the Eid prayer. Then he recites.

When the prayer is done, we sit quietly for the *khutba*. It's just as important, and we must not talk. Not yet. Mom has brought some cars and crackers for my baby brother. But I sit quietly, my hands folded in my lap, trying to keep my mind on what the Imam says. I'm not a baby.

It takes a long time. Sometimes I think of what my classmates must be doing in school, and I smile. I'm glad it's Eid.

When the khutba is done, we hug again. Then we mingle and meet our family and friends. Hugs and more hugs. "Eid Mubarak! What a wonderful day! We buy cotton candy and helium balloons. The baby laughs, his face all sticky.

The crowd is huge. So many Muslims in one place. I feel safe. Happy.

After a while we gather at the car. Then we drive home, but not to stay. We just stop in to pick up the presents, and the cake Mom baked. Then we go to Grandma's house, where everyone gathers. Uncles and aunts, cousins and more cousins. Everyone in their nicest clothes.

It's Eid-ul-Fitr and time for presents. What a mess! Wrapping paper and packaging all over the place. Grandma spoils us. She always buys so much. Mom is smiling. Dad is grinning.

We eat and eat and eat some more. Pineapple tarts and cupcakes, chocolate and toffee, curry and rice, baked chicken and *daal puri*. It feels strange after Ramadan to be eating in the daytime. Even the sun looks happy that it's Eid.

daal puri: flat bread filled with ground chickpeas, commonly made by West Indians

We tell stories. Of past Eids and the funny things that happened. Of Cousin Ruhal, when he was five, how he stepped on his pizza and messed up his sock. And everyone laughs and laughs as if it had just happened. Cousin Ruhal laughs too, even though he's a little embarrassed.

Then my cousins and I go into Grandpa's old shed, our secret clubhouse, and have a meeting of our secret club. We sneak food from the table and carry it to the clubhouse, and while we laugh and tell secrets and jokes and riddles, we munch on candies and cupcakes and chips and pretzels. And wash it all down with some pop.

And everyone admires the way Grandma has decorated the house. With balloons and streamers and signs saying "Happy Eid!" And Grandma smiles and blushes, telling everyone to have more candy.

At the end of the day, when we've visited everybody, and we're tired and still full, and the car is crammed with gifts, we head home. The stars twinkle and shine. Like they're happy, too.

We put our pretty clothes in the laundry to be washed. I tried but couldn't keep my dress clean. "That's all right," says Mom.

The next day is school. I go lugging a big bag. It's full of little sacks of candy, one for each kid in the class. We don't celebrate Halloween or birthdays, so we share our joy at Eid. The kids at school are excited. Eid is fun for them, too. Even the teacher knows I have a treat for her. Mom made pineapple tarts and a packet of goodies.

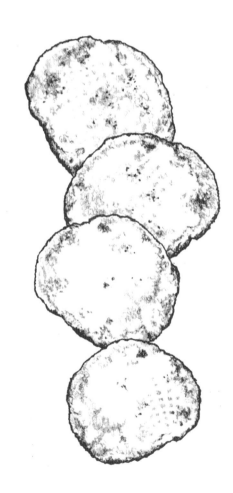

I feel proud, giving out my little sacks of candies. And I have a few extra for my friends in the other classes.

Sometimes at Christmas or Hanukkah or Halloween, my friends ask me if I don't miss the fun they're having. But I just smile and shake my head. They have Christmas. They have Hanukkah and Halloween. I have Eid-ul-Fitr and Eid-ul-Adha. Two Eids to look forward to. They're more than enough for me.

Eid Mubarak: above is the Arabic writing for Eid Mubarak. Arabic is the language that the Quran was revealed in. It is written and read from right to left.

AFTER EVERY HARDSHIP
THERE IS EASE,
AND AFTER RAMADAN
THERE IS EID.

35

SAYINGS OF
PROPHET MUHAMMAD
(Peace be upon him)

The person is not a proper Muslim
who eats till he is full
but leaves his neighbours hungry.

No man is a true believer
unless he wants for his brother that
which he wants for himself.

What actions are most excellent?
To gladden the heart of human beings,
to feed the hungry,
to help the afflicted,
to lighten the sorrow of the sorrowful,
and to remove the sufferings of the injured.

SAMOSAS!

(PAKISTAN)

Mr. Kareem is coming today. All the kids are excited, and I can't blame them. He always brings a *sadaqa* for us. Today we are expecting special treats. Some people say it's because he was once an orphan too, long ago. But I think it's just because he's so kind.

Often he brings his wife. She's the plumpest lady I've ever seen—she looks like a walking pillow. Or a cloud. Like she'll just float away. And she's so nice. Always smiling. Her eyes shine with gentleness. Too bad she never had children. She'd be a great mother.

"Ahmad!" I sit up. The teacher, Mr. Feroz, is looking at me. "Dreaming again? What did I just say?"

There's no clue on the dusty chalkboard. He could have been talking about anything. I shrug.

"Come here." I shuffle up to the front. I know what's coming. I always get it.

Grab your ears. I do. "No. No. With your hands through your legs, grab your ears."

I'm cramped, with my arms wound through my legs, grabbing my ears.

"Now, stay that way."

sadaqa: charity. The treats that Mr. Kareem brings for the orphan children are one of many ways Muslims practice charity. In addition to everyday kindnesses and acts of charity, Muslims have to give 2.5 per cent of their annual savings to help the poor and needy. This is known as zakaat.

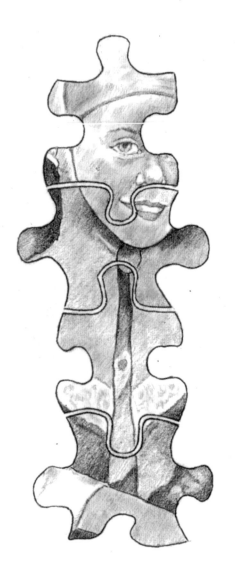

pakoras: fried dumplings

ludoos: round yellow sweets

gelabis: orange sticky sweets

Mr. Feroz continues the lesson. Some kids are snickering. I feel like a fool.

I should be used to this uncomfortable position. I'm in it enough.

I wonder what Mr. Kareem will bring. I hope it's *pakoras*, or maybe *ludoos* or *gelabis*. Or maybe... My stomach growls so loudly everyone can hear it.

Mr. Feroz scowls at me. "Ahmad! No talking."

"It wasn't me," I mumble. "It's my stomach." All the kids burst out laughing.

Mr. Feroz is furious. "Get to your seat then and keep quiet."

"Yes, sir." But I can't help wondering what the treat will be. There's never enough food here in the orphanage. My stomach's still grumbling. I give it a punch to stop it. It quiets down a bit. Still an hour till lunch.

When class is finally over, we're let outside to play in the courtyard until lunch is ready. I gallop around the corner and crash right into a potbelly. Looking up, I see it's Mr. Kareem. I open my mouth to say something, but nothing comes out. And, just my luck, Mr. Feroz saw the whole thing. He rushes up and grabs me by the shoulder.

"I'm so sorry, Mr. Kareem. This silly Ahmad. He never watches where he's going. Always absent-minded he is. Beg pardon." I'm so embarrassed. My face is hot. Why'd he have to tell Mr. Kareem that? Now he knows about me, and I wish he didn't.

Mr. Kareem laughs. My ears burn at the sound of it. I wish I was anywhere else. "That's all right," he says. "I used to be in a big hurry myself. Now I take my time."

He smiles at me. And it seems like he's not mad, or disappointed. Which would be worse. And before I know it, I'm smiling back.

Mr. Feroz is talking. He says, "Of course, you can take your time now. You're a wealthy businessman. We must teach these children manners, especially Ahmad here. He's slow to learn."

Again my face is hot, and I'm embarrassed. Why does he always have to pick on me? Other kids do bad things too. How come he only sees it when I do bad things?

Mr. Kareem is frowning. He must be displeased. Mr. Feroz takes him by the arm, "Come, sir. The superintendent would love to meet with you."

I'm forgotten. Standing there while all the other kids are playing in the yard. Funny, but I don't feel like playing anymore.

What if I try harder? What if I were to be good? Would they even believe me? Or would they think I'm playing another trick? If only I wasn't so bad. Then the teacher wouldn't have told Mr. Kareem all those awful things about me.

For lunch we have *daal* and rice. The daal is thin, the rice is sticky. But it fills me up. A little. And then it's time for *Zuhr* prayer.

Most of the boys only pretend to make *wudu*. Usually I'd be one of them, just pretending too. But today is different. I make it properly. And I hope Mr. Feroz sees me doing it. But he doesn't. I even take my time so he will look my way, but he's busy with someone else. Oh, well. At least I know I made it properly.

Then we go to pray. Most of the boys are too busy nudging each other and stepping on each other's toes to concentrate on praying. And usually I do that, too. I guess I really was bad. I'm starting to see all the things I do wrong. But this prayer time, even though the boys beside me keep nudging and shoving, I don't shove back. I pray properly. But no one notices.

I knew it! After lunch Mr. Kareem is standing at the front of the prayer hall with a large sack. Mmm. *Samosas.* With meat! My favourite. There are big ones and little ones. And I'm at the end of the line. Everyone is grabbing the biggest ones they can find. Pushing and shoving. I would be, too, but I'm on my best behaviour. Waiting my turn. By the time

daal: split pea

Zuhr: one of the five daily prayers. It is prayed shortly after midday.

wudu: a washing performed before the prayer

samosas: an East Indian deep-fried dish consisting of spicy meat or vegetables in pastry. There is a recipe for samosas on page 42.

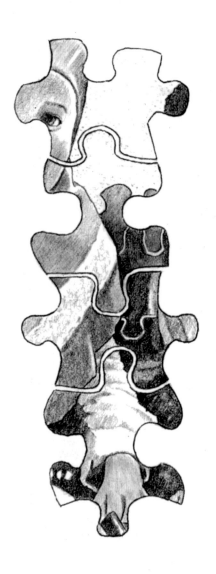

I get up there, there's only one small samosa left. Hardly a mouthful. My eyes burn. I want to cry. Being good is so hard! But I take it. I do remember my manners. I do! But before I can say thank you, that same Mr. Feroz reminds me. I want to scream, I'm so mad. But that will just get me in trouble, so I don't. I just say, "Thank you, Mr. Kareem."

There's a gleam in Mr. Kareem's eyes, and he smiles widely at me. "You're most welcome, Ahmad."

He remembers my name! Somehow the anger is gone.

I take a big bite of the samosa and almost lose my tooth. Ow! There's something wrong. Something hard in my mouth. Not a bone. Metal. I fish it out. It's a gold coin! So valuable! What a grand amount it would fetch in the marketplace! What should I do? It must have fallen into the mixture by mistake. It must belong to Mr. Kareem. But he's so rich, would he even know it is missing?

I had promised I'd try to be good. But that was before I found this! If only I'd promised after. But I can't keep it. I need to show Mr. Feroz, show myself that I'm a good boy. Not a bad boy as he thinks I am. So I take it back up to Mr. Kareem. Tap on his arm and say he must have lost it.

Mr. Kareem looks funny, like he wants to cry. He hugs me hard. My ear rubs against a button on his vest, but it still feels good. It's been so long since anyone hugged me.

He's babbling to the teacher. Saying he will *adopt* me. I can't believe what's happening.

He said that he's been wanting to adopt a child, waiting for one who would return the money he hid in the treats. There was other money?

I can't believe it. Mr. Feroz tries to convince him to take another boy, but Mr. Kareem is firm. He refuses. He wants an honest boy. He wants me!!

adoption: When Muslims adopt children, they are required to protect the origin and lineage of the child. The child therefore keeps the name of his or her father.

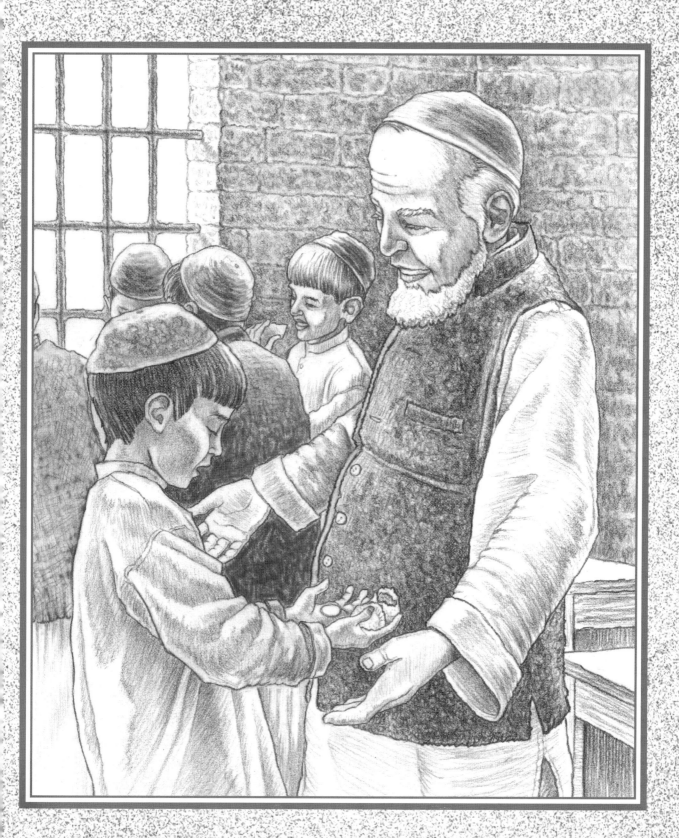

HOW TO MAKE SAMOSAS
FOR YOUR FAMILY
OR FOR YOUR FRIENDS

INGREDIENTS

1 lb ground beef
2 tbsp lemon juice
1/2 tsp crushed garlic
1/2 tsp crushed ginger
1/2 tsp salt
1 finely chopped onion
1/2 tsp cayenne pepper
pre-made pastry wrappers (check your nearest Indian food store)

To make paste
2 tbsp all-purpose flour
3 tbsp water

3 cups of oil for deep-frying

METHOD

Cook the ground beef on medium heat
with lemon juice, garlic, ginger, salt, onion and cayenne pepper,
until the meat starts to turn brown.
When the meat is completely cooked, drain the fat very well.
Let the mixture cool.
Mix the flour and water to make the paste.

Fold the wrappers to make a cone and fill with the meat.
Seal each cone with the paste.
Deep-fry the samosas in the oil (not too hot).
Cook on medium and turn often until golden brown.
Drain or blot dry and serve.

EID MUBARAK

HOW TO MAKE AN EID CARD
FOR YOUR FAMILY
OR FOR YOUR FRIENDS

You will need   1 sheet of tracing paper, 1 sheet of regular white paper, wrapping paper (ask Mom if she has a few leftover pieces), some sort of stiff board such as Bristol board or the cardboard from a shirt box, coloured pencils, 1 regular pencil, and glue

1) Centre your tracing paper over the Arabic writing to the right. Trace with a dark coloured pencil.
2) Use a regular pencil to indicate lightly the fold line which will be underneath the writing when you turn it the right way.
3) Fold your tracing paper along the fold line. The Arabic writing is now on the inside. Rub vigorously with your fist and open the paper. You should see a mirror image appearing.
4) When you can see it all, erase your fold line and trace Eid Mubarak (as above). It goes between the two lines of Arabic writing. Did you know that to read Arabic, you must start from the right and finish towards the left?
5) Cut a rectangle around your drawing. Leave about an inch of white tracing paper all around the Arabic writing. Paste this to another rectangle of the regular paper, the same size, to strengthen it.
6) Take your Bristol board or shirt-box board and make a folding card like the ones shown above. Make the card backing big enough so that you have an inch or more of space all around your drawing. Centre your drawing on the front and paste it down.
7) Make a border with your wrapping paper and paste it down around the drawing. To finish, use your coloured pencils to shade in the text. It's often nice to choose colours from the wrapping paper frame, but that is up to you!

SAYINGS OF
PROPHET MUHAMMAD
(Peace be upon him)

There is a polish to take away rust from everything;
and the polish of the heart
is the remembrance of God.

God, the Almighty, has laid down religious duties,
so do not neglect them;
He has set boundaries,
so do not overstep them;
He has prohibited some things,
so do not violate them;
about some things He was silent—out of
compassion for you, not forgetfulness—
so do not seek after them.

JUMBO JELLY SHOES
(ENGLAND)

Jameelah and her little sister, Aisha, had been a long time in the sweet shop. Aisha said, "Which sweets are you going to buy? The Jumbo Jelly Shoes or the Chocolate Blaster Balls?"

Jameelah frowned. All the sweets looked so good. How could she ever decide? She looked down at the fifty pence in the palm of her hand. It was all that was left of her allowance, and it was only Monday.

Aisha grabbed a packet of Jumbo Jelly Shoes. The wrapper crinkled loudly in her little fist. She held out her chubby hand. "Do I have enough?" Two twenty pence and a grubby ten pence.

Jameelah nodded.

But Aisha hardly noticed. She squealed as she caught sight of some Sour Poodle Doo. "I've just got to have this." Pouting, she stared at the money in her hand. "Can I get both?"

Jameelah sighed. She knew how her sister felt. "No, Aisha, you can only get one or the other."

The store owner watched them, his hairy arms crossed and his foot tapping the floor.

"Come on, Aisha. We have to get going. We have to choose." Aisha settled on the Sour Poodle Doo. Jameelah closed her eyes and grabbed a packet. It was Jumbo Jelly Shoes. She kind of wished it was

45

Lard, gelatin and mono and diglycerides: pig meat and any of its byproducts such as lard, gelatin and mono and diglycerides are among the foods prohibited by God for Muslims to eat.

the Chocolate Blaster Balls, but it was too late to change it now. Besides, she'd heard they were good. The store owner was coming toward them.

Jameelah went to the counter feeling as though she'd forgotten to do something. While she and Aisha handed over the money, a thought nagged at the edge of her mind. She was definitely forgetting something, but what? She shrugged. It couldn't be that important.

Before they were even out the door, Aisha tore open her packet and chose a blue lump of Poodle Doo. Then Jameelah remembered what she'd forgotten to do. She grabbed the packet. "Wait, Aisha..."

She'd forgotten to check the ingredients. It was almost six o'clock. The store owner was right behind them, ushering them out so he could lock the door.

Aisha was just about to pop the blue lump in her mouth when Jameelah snatched it out of her hand. Aisha cried, "Why'd you do that? That's mine!"

Jameelah read the ingredients. *No lard, no gelatin, no mono and diglycerides.* Just some fancy chemicals with a lot of letters like EDTA and FD & C. "It's okay," she said, handing the packet back to her, "you can eat it."

Then she read her packet of Jumbo Jelly Shoes. There were the dreaded words. Gelatin, lard, mono and diglycerides. They were all there. She turned around and pounded on the glass door. The store owner came with a scowl on his face.

"What you want now?"

"I want to change this packet."

"Store closed. Go away."

In an instant, the man was gone into a back storeroom. It was no use. Jameelah had wasted her last fifty pence on something she couldn't eat.

Aisha tugged on her sleeve. Jameelah looked down to see her chewing on a wad of blue Poodle Doo. Her lips were blue, her teeth were blue, her

tongue was blue. Even the fingertips of her right hand were blue. "What's the matter, Jameelah? Why don't you eat your sweets?"

"They've got got pig stuff in them."

Aisha reached for the packet. "I'll eat it."

Jameelah yanked the packet out of reach. "You can't."

Aisha popped some more Poodle Doo in her mouth and said, "Why not?"

"We can't eat pig stuff. It's against *Islam.*"

"But Mum and Dad won't know."

Jameelah sighed. *Allah* would know. His *angels* were probably writing it down this very moment. She glanced at her shoulders as if she could see the invisible beings perched there, writing down all her good and bad deeds to show Allah on the *Day of Judgment.*

Aisha had finished all the Poodle Doo. "Go on, Jameelah. Eat it. I won't tell."

Jameelah laughed. She wouldn't fall for that. "I'll just throw it out."

"Let me," said Aisha, licking her lips.

Jameelah laughed again. "It's okay. I'll get rid of it when we get home."

But when they got home, their parents hustled them in, asking why they'd taken so long. It was time for supper. Aisha forgot all about the Jumbo Jelly Shoes, but Jameelah didn't. She wished she could forget about them. But while she ate her soup, she could feel the bulge in her pocket.

She should throw the sweets away. But wasn't that wasting food? And money? And wasn't wasting a sin?

What if she just didn't buy them next time? If she'd just eaten them and read the package afterward, she wouldn't have to feel like this. It would have been a mistake and Allah wouldn't punish her for it. Why did she have to read the packet anyway?

After dinner, Aisha sidled up to her. "Did you

throw away the Jumbo Jelly Shoes?"

"Not yet."

"Why don't you just taste them. I bet they're good."

"They probably are."

"If you give me some, I won't tell on you."

"Aisha!"

"C'mon."

Jameelah stiffened. "Allah will be angry."

"Just a little bit doesn't matter."

"If it didn't matter, Allah wouldn't have forbidden it." At that moment, their mother called Aisha. Jameelah was relieved. Aisha was very convincing.

But now that she was alone, her eyes were glued to the Jelly Shoes. They looked delicious. Her mouth watered so much she had to swallow. It would be a shame to waste them, a shame. She would never buy them again. Before she could change her mind she crammed a handful in her mouth.

They were so tangy, the spots beneath her ears tingled.

She felt very wicked, shoved the rest of the packet in her pocket and quickly swallowed. But the sweets made such a wad that they hurt her throat going down. She finished just in time.

Aisha came back. "Where're the sweets?"

"I flushed them down the toilet," said Jameelah.

"Oh," said Aisha, looking disappointed. She trudged away to play.

Jameelah's stomach hurt. It was tight, as if someone had tied it in a knot. She went and lay down, but it didn't help. Her mother came to check on her later and found her holding her stomach in pain.

"What's the matter?"

"Nothing," said Jameelah, wishing she'd never heard of Jumbo Jelly Shoes. They hadn't even tasted that good.

When, after a while, she still felt no better, her mother took her to the doctor.

"I don't understand it," said Jameelah's mother. "Do you think it could be food poisoning?"

The doctor put the stethoscope against her stomach and listened. "Sounds like a nervous tummy. Everything seems fine. Maybe she ate something that didn't agree with her."

Jameelah touched her pocket where the rest of the Jelly Shoes were. She knew what she had to do.

When she got home, she marched into the bathroom and flushed them down the toilet.

Immediately, her stomach felt a lot better.

GLIMPSES FROM THE LIFE OF PROPHET MUHAMMAD (PEACE BE UPON HIM)

The Prophet Muhammad (peace be upon him) was born in Mecca in 570 A.D. His mother's name was Aminah, and his father's name was Abdullah, but his father died while he was in his mother's womb.

HIS AGE	EVENTS IN HIS LIFE
age 6	His mother Aminah dies. His grandfather Abdul Muttalib takes care of him.
age 8	His grandfather dies. His uncle Abu Talib takes care of him from then on.
age 25	He marries Khadijah, his first wife. She is 40 years-old at the time. Together they have four daughters and two sons. Their two sons die in childhood.
age 40	In 610 A.D., he is chosen by God to be His final Prophet. He receives the first revelation of the Quran through Angel Gabriel. Revelation continues for the next twenty-three years.
age 45	Due to opposition and oppression imposed on his followers, he advises a group of Muslims to emigrate to Abyssinia (615 A.D.). He believes that the Negus, the Christian king at the time, will protect them. The king does, but there follows a two-year social and economic boycott against Prophet Muhammad (peace be upon him) and his followers who had stayed in Mecca.
age 53	There is a conspiracy amongst Meccan leaders to kill Prophet Muhammad (peace be upon him). This results in The Hijra, the migration from Mecca to Medina in 622 A.D. This migration marks the beginning of the Islamic Calendar.
age 55	The Battle of Badr takes place in 624 A.D., the first battle between Muslims and non-Muslims. Revelation comes from God to change the direction that Muslims face during prayer from Jerusalem to the Kaaba in Mecca. Other battles follow in subsequent years.
age 59	He attempts to perform Hajj, a pilgrimage to Mecca, but he is refused by the Meccans. This results in the Treaty of Hudaibiya (628 A.D.). He sends invitation to kings and rulers inviting them to Islam. Amongst them are the leaders of the Persian and Byzantine Empires.
age 61	After being away for eight years, in 630 A.D., he makes a triumphant return to Mecca.
age 63	He performs his only Hajj and delivers his farewell sermon. Prophet Muhammad (peace be upon him) dies a few months later, in 632 A.D.

SURAH AL-FIL (THE ELEPHANT)

Chapter 105 of the Quran

In the Name of God, the Most Beneficent,
the Most Merciful

1.

Have you not seen how your Lord dealt with the
owners of the elephant?

2.

Did He not make their plot go astray?

3.

And sent against them birds, in flocks,

4.

Striking them with stones of sijjil.

5.

And made them like an empty field of stalks (of
which the corn has been eaten up by cattle).

THE YEAR OF THE ELEPHANT
(NIGERIA)

*H*alima was confused. She checked one book and then the other. And then she checked the first again. She didn't want to go to her grandmother; she never just answered a question. But she needed to know, and Grandmother was the only one home. Desperate, she finally went to her. At least, she would know the answer.

"Grandmother, when was *Prophet Muhammad* (peace be upon him) born? In one book it says 570 A.D. and in another it says 571. Don't they know for sure?"

Her grandmother smiled, showing many missing teeth. She set Halima onto her knee and said, "No one knows for sure the exact date the Prophet Muhammad (peace be upon him) was born. It depends on which tribe you ask. You see, back then, the Arabian tribes liked nothing better than to be fighting each other. But there were four sacred months when all fighting was forbidden. Sometimes, when a tribe was winning a war just before a sacred month was coming, they'd change the name of the month so they could keep on fighting and winning. It became a terrible mess. Each tribe had a different calendar, and although they still had four sacred months, no one outside that tribe knew exactly when they'd be.

"So all the months and years around that time were confused together. But we do know that Prophet Muhammad (peace be upon him) was born in the Year of the Elephant. It was called the Year of

Prophet Muhammad (peace be upon him): last prophet of Islam. The Quran mentions the names of twenty-five prophets, but there were many more, including Abraham, Moses and Jesus. Muslims believe that all nations received prophets from God. These prophets were from within their communities and all of them invited to "Islam," which means "finding peace by obeying God," Prophet Muhammad (peace be upon him) is considered to be the last prophet of Islam.

the Elephant for a very good reason."

There was a twinkle in her grandmother's eye. Halima knew grandmother wanted to tell her a story, but Halima had to finish her homework. But without the birthdate! Maybe she'd hurry up. So Halima said, "All right, Grandmother, why was it called the Year of the Elephant?"

"I'm glad you asked. Way back, a long time before Prophet Muhammad (peace be upon him) was born, a long time before the Year of the Elephant, there lived Prophet Abraham and his son, Prophet Ishmael (peace be upon them). They built a house of God in the barren valley of *Mecca*. They called it the *Kaaba*, which means "cube", because it looked like a cube. All the *Arabs*, every year for years and years afterward, in fact to this very day, came to visit this house of God.

"What made the Kaaba so special was that it was a sanctuary—a safe place. A sanctuary in a sacred city, Mecca. In all of Mecca, and even for a few miles around it, no one was allowed to hurt anyone else, or hurt animals or even hurt a blade of grass. It was as if there was a magical circle, a boundary around Mecca, where everyone and everything was safe. This area was called the Haram. If people wanted to fight, they had to go outside the Haram to do so.

"Now way down south in the land of Yemen, there lived a man named Abraha. He wasn't a king, but he ruled Yemen on behalf of a king. At that time, Yemen was under the rule of an Abyssinian king, an African Christian king, called the Negus. It was he who'd set Abraha to rule Yemen."

Halima interrupted. "I didn't know there were African kings."

Her grandmother nodded. "Yes, child. Now listen. Abraha was an ambitious man. He knew that long ago Yemen had been a great and marvellous land. Rich and glorious. A land of frankincense and myrrh. In fact, during the days of Prophet *Solomon* (peace be upon him), it wasn't called Yemen at all.

Mecca: today a city in Saudi Arabia. It is here that Prophet Muhammad (peace be upon him) was born, in the year of the Elephant.

Arabs: a common misconception is that Muslims are Arabs. A Muslim may be Arab, but can also be West Indian, Chinese, Russian, American, Indonesian, Canadian, British, or any other nationality. On the other hand, an Arab could be a Muslim, a Jew, a Christian, an atheist, or of any religion. While there are one billion Muslims in the world, there are only about 200 million Arabs. Arab Muslims therefore only make up about 20 per cent of the Muslim population of the world.

Kaaba: considered the first house of God. It was built by Prophets Abraham and his son Ishmael (peace be upon them). It is located in Mecca, Saudi Arabia. It is toward the Kaaba that Muslims around the world face when they stand in prayer.

It was called Sheba and was ruled by the beautiful *Queen of Sheba*, who was mentioned in the Bible itself. Abraha wanted to make Yemen great again. And he was jealous. Jealous of the love the Arabs had for the Kaaba. He wanted to make a house of God so magnificent that the Arabs wouldn't bother going to the Kaaba anymore, but instead would come to Yemen, and with them they'd bring their money. Yemen would be rich once again.

"So Abraha built a magnificent cathedral. He took the marble from one of the Queen of Sheba's ruined palaces and used it to build his splendid cathedral. In it, he placed crosses of gold and silver and pulpits of ivory and ebony. It truly was a sight to behold.

"Then he wrote to his king, the Negus, and said, 'I have built thee a church, O King, the like of which was never built for any king before thee; and I shall not rest until I have diverted unto it the pilgrimage of the Arabs.' But he didn't have the sense to keep this ambition to himself. He bragged about it to anyone who'd listen.

"But the Arabs still preferred the Kaaba, even though it wasn't anywhere near as fancy as Abraha's cathedral. They still went to the Kaaba for pilgrimage. And with them went their money.

"That the Arabs still loved the Kaaba, even though he'd worked so hard on his cathedral, made Abraha even more jealous. And when people are jealous, they do stupid things.

"The Arabs had heard the boast of Abraha and were angry. And when people are angry, they also do stupid things. In fact, they were so angry that a man from the tribe of Banu Kinanah came to Yemen one night just to defile the cathedral, and when he was done, he ran home to his tribe, safely.

"They say he defiled the cathedral by pooping in it."

Halima laughed out loud. "Didn't they have bathrooms?"

"Of course not. They went to the bathroom outside, in the bushes. Anyway, Abraha was furious.

Solomon (peace be upon him): a wise king of the nation of Israel and a Prophet of God.

Queen of Sheba: according to Muslim tradition, her name was Bilqis, and she ruled a fine kingdom. Sheba is the old name for Yemen, a rich land at the time of Solomon (peace be upon him). By the time Prophet Muhammad (peace be upon him) was born, Yemen had declined in wealth and prestige.

55

Absolutely consumed with rage. How dared this Arab do such a thing as to poop in his cathedral!

"Now, it would have made sense for Abraha to chase down this man and punish him. It would even have made sense for Abraha to confront the tribe of Kinanah to pay for defiling the cathedral. But Abraha did not do this. Instead he saw the perfect opportunity to get rid of his rival, the Kaaba. The Arabs would not come to the cathedral for pilgrimage, because they went to the Kaaba. But if he were to destroy the Kaaba...

"Yes, he decided. That would be his revenge! Then they would come, pilgrims in droves, and with them would come their money. Yemen would be rich and glorious once again.

"So Abraha gathered a mighty army, the likes of which has seldom been seen, and in the front, in the very vanguard, he placed a mighty beast... an elephant.

"The Arabs rode camels and horses and sometimes they rode donkeys and mules. But everyone knows that camels and horses and donkeys and mules are no match for an elephant! There was no Arab army that could stop Abraha, even though some of them tried. And as he came north, he grew bolder and bolder. And he captured whatever riches he could find along the way.

"Among the plunder, Abraha captured two hundred camels that belonged to a very special man named *Abdul Muttalib* who lived in Mecca.

"The people of Mecca held a council of war and decided it was useless to try to stop Abraha.

"When Abraha had made camp just outside the Haram, he sent a message to the people of Mecca, telling them that he hadn't come there to kill anyone. Only to destroy the house of God. And he asked them to send him their chief.

"Of all the men in Mecca, Abdul Muttalib was the wisest, and the closest to being the chief. So they all decided Abdul Muttalib should go.

Abdul Muttalib: the grandfather of Prophet Muhammad (peace be upon him)

"When Abraha saw Abdul Muttalib, he was quite impressed. He got up from his fancy chair, the only chair in the tent, to greet Abdul Muttalib. And then Abraha sat down on the carpet beside him, so they could speak as equals. Abraha asked Abdul Muttalib if he had any favours to ask. Abdul Muttalib said that he wanted his two hundred camels back.

"Abraha was surprised that at such a time this man should be thinking of his camels instead of what Abraha would do to God's house, and he said so.

"Abdul Muttalib said: 'I am the lord of the camels, and the Kaaba likewise has a Lord Who Will Defend it.'

"Abraha said, 'God cannot defend it against me.'

'We shall see,' said Abdul Muttalib, 'But give me my camels.'

"Abraha gave him his camels and Abdul Muttalib went back to Mecca and warned all the people to leave the city and head for higher ground. Then Abdul Muttalib went to the Kaaba and prayed to God for help. He grabbed the metal ring of the Kaaba door and cried, 'O God, your servant protects his house, You protect Your House.'

"The very next day, Abraha got his troops ready to march into Mecca, but it seems they had reached that invisible boundary that marked the sanctuary around Mecca—the Haram. When the elephant was brought to the front of the army, instead of proceeding forward, he sat down. He would not budge. Not even when Abraha's soldiers stuck him with spears and hit him with iron bars around the head. Some of the men in the ranks knew it was a bad omen."

"Oh, the poor elephant," said Halima.

"Abraha should have realized. He should have turned around and gone home while he still could. But nothing would stop him from destroying the Kaaba. He was that jealous of it. And nothing would take away his revenge. So he decided to trick the elephant. He turned his troops around and pretended to go back toward Yemen. The

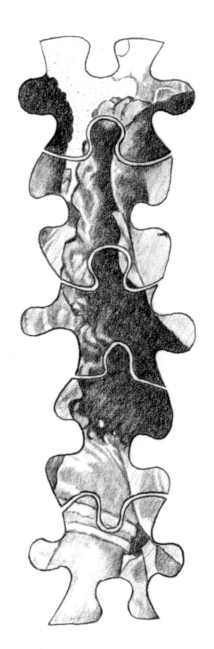

elephant got up and started back with them. After a few steps however, Abraha turned them back toward Mecca, and the elephant sat down again.

"If only Abraha had truly gone. But in a moment it was too late.

"In the West the sky grew black. And slowly the blackness grew nearer and nearer. And with it came a strange sound—like a wave from the sea, on its way to destroy them. But it was not a wave. It was a flock of birds. Actually, it was more like a cloud of birds. And each bird held three stones, one in its beak and one in each of its claws. They were stones made of a special kind of clay—the kind potters use and fire in a kiln to make pottery. These stones were just that hard and sharp. They swooped down on the army and let go of their stones. And they were going so fast and the stones hit with such force that they pierced the coats of armour the soldiers wore. Every stone hit a man, and where it hit, the skin began to rot.

"There was panic and devastation everywhere."

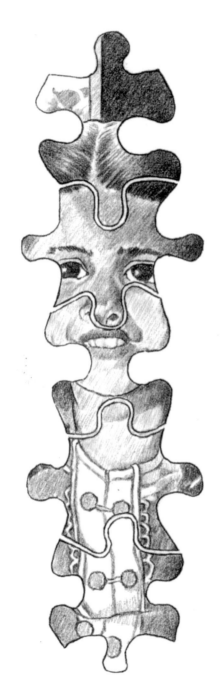

"Devastation, Grandmother?"

"It means everything was ruined. Most of the army was in tatters, like dried-up leaves, broken and crushed. And those who still lived quickly turned back toward Yemen. Almost all of them died before getting to Yemen and were buried along the way. Abraha died after he got back to Yemen.

"But not everyone was hurt. The elephant was spared."

"Oh, I'm glad," said Halima. "I didn't want the elephant to get hurt."

"Not one stone had hit him. Almost as if the birds knew that the elephant was not to blame. And some of the men were spared, too. As if the birds had been told which of the men had been forced to come along and hadn't wanted to damage God's house at all.

"Those men didn't bother going back to Yemen. They stayed near Mecca, where they made their homes and earned their livelihood herding sheep.

"It was a magnificent year, the Year of the Elephant. The people of Mecca, the tribe of Qureysh, were thereafter called the 'People of God' because everyone thought God had come to their defense.

"But before the Year of the Elephant was over, the 'People of God' were to get another gift from Him.

"About fifty days after the defeat of Abraha, a grandson was born to Abdul Muttalib. The baby was named 'Muhammad', a name never heard before (but often heard since). It means 'Someone worth praising'. And forty years later, Muhammad (peace be upon him) was to become the last Prophet of Islam. And although they don't know exactly which month or year it was, they do know he was born in the Year of the Elephant."

Halima said, "But I can't write 'Muhammad (peace be upon him) was born in the Year of the Elephant.' The teacher wants a date."

"Oh," said her grandmother. "Then write that he was born on the 22nd of April, 570 A.D."

60

"Thanks," said Halima. And she went back to finish her project. Grandmother could have just said so.

When she handed in her project the next day, the teacher frowned. "Actually, Halima," she said, "nobody knows for sure what year the Prophet (peace be upon him) was born. But they do know he was born..."

"In the Year of the Elephant!" thought Halima. It turned out she lost two marks for not writing that.

SURAH AL-HAJJ
(THE PILGRIMAGE)
Chapter 22, verses 26 – 29
of the Quran

And remember when we showed Abraham
the site of the Sacred House at Mecca saying:
"Associate not anything in worship with Me; and sanctify
My house for those who circle it, and those who stand,
or bow, or prostrate themselves there in prayer.
And proclaim to mankind the Hajj (pilgrimage).
They will come on foot and on every kind of camel
lean on account of journeys,
through deep and distant mountain highways.
That they may witness the benefits provided for them,
and mention the Name of God
on appointed days over the cattle
which He has provided for them for sacrifice:
then eat thereof and with it feed the distressed poor.
Then let them complete the rites prescribed for them,
perform their vows and again circle
the Ancient House (The Kaaba)."

LOST AT HAJJ
(SAUDI ARABIA)

*I*t's the worst place in the world to get lost, and the worst time too.

I'm huddled in a forgotten corner of the Great Mosque in *Mecca*. All hope is gone. I will never see my mother and father again.

A shuffling step on the cool marble tiles. An old man smiles down at me.

I don't smile back. What's the point? He won't speak English; they speak Arabic here. As I expected, the old man mumbles in Arabic. I shrug. He tries another language. I shrug again. Finally he says, "Are you lost?"

To be able to understand! I jump to my feet, nodding.

"Where are your parents?"

"I don't know."

The old man nods. "Come, we will search for them."

So I walk beside him. My feet are sore, but I ignore them.

I learn his name is Abdullah, and he came for *Hajj,* many years ago, and didn't have the heart to leave. So he applied for a job cleaning the Great Mosque. He says it is an honour to sweep God's house.

And I tell him my name is Bilal.

Mecca: today a city in Saudi Arabia. It is here that Prophet Muhammad (peace be upon him) was born, in the year of the Elephant.

Hajj: a pillar of Islam that every Muslim must perform at least once in their lifetime, if they can afford it. It involves visiting the Kaaba and other sites in and around Mecca that are of significance to Muslims.

63

I ask, "Are you making hajj?"

The old man smiles. "Maybe, *Insha Allah*. I may get time to go to *Arafat*."

When he says Arafat, it reminds me. "I have a dream," I say, before I can stop myself.

"What is it?"

I feel foolish. "Never mind."

"You can tell me. I won't laugh."

As we walk I tell him. "I've always dreamed of giving the *adhan* at Arafat. In front of all the people gathered."

He does not laugh. Gently he says, "But they do not give the adhan for everyone. There are too many to pray together."

"Oh," I say. My dream is gone. I shouldn't have told him. I want only to find my mother and father and get away.

He smiles. "Your dream suits you. The first Bilal was an African slave set free. And the first to call to prayer."

That's why it is my dream.

We search the old hills of *Safa* and *Marwa* again. Thousands and thousands of faces. Walking. Running. Men dressed like me, in two pieces of white cloth. Everyone alike. I can't tell a beggar from a king.

An hour passes and then another. I have already done this. We search all three floors of the Great Mosque. Again. My legs are aching, and my eyes are blurry from looking closely at so many faces.

The old man is tired, too. I see him stumble. And when I urge him to rest, he doesn't argue.

"Don't worry," he says. But there's a frown in his eyes. "We'll find them, Insha Allah."

Insha Allah. If God wills.

My stomach grumbles so loudly, it startles me. And the old man chuckles. "Let's find something to eat."

By the time we've eaten and drunk, the sun is gone. We return to the Great Mosque in time for prayer.

muezzin: the person who calls the adhan, the call to prayer.

Maghrib: one of the five daily prayers, prayed shortly after sunset

Kaaba: a cube-shaped building, the house of God, that Muslims around the world face when they stand for prayer. It is located in Mecca, Saudi Arabia. It was rebuilt by Abraham and his son Ishmael, and is considered the first house of God.

Fajr: one of the five daily prayers for Muslims. It is prayed before sunrise.

Abraham: a prophet of God and the father of prophethood. Moses, Jesus, and Muhammad (peace be upon him) are all descended from him.

Mina: the plain where Abraham took Ishmael to sacrifice him according to a vision from God. The sacrifice was a test of obedience for Abraham, the father, and Ishmael, the son. But before Abraham could carry it through, God ransomed Ishmael with a ram, which Abraham sacrificed, in his stead. To commemorate the sacrifice that Abraham and Ishmael were willing to make, pilgrims also sacrifice an animal. And the meat is distributed to the poor. This is the day of Eid ul Adha for the rest of the Muslim world. Muslims around the world also sacrifice an animal (a sheep, cow, or goat) and give part of it to the poor in their neighbourhoods.

I hear the *muezzin* call the adhan for *Maghrib,* and I stop. A magical moment for me. I stand perfectly still, hardly breathing. I call the adhan with him. Word for word. Just as well as he can. The old man watches.

When we pray, I ask God to help. Help me find my mother and my father.

The crowds have thinned. A little. We look down into the crowded courtyard and across to the *Kaaba.* As if we could spot them in all the crowds.

I must keep looking, but I'm tired. I've been walking all day. I could lie down on the marble floor and fall asleep in a minute. Abdullah says, "Come stay with me and my wife. I cannot let you sleep here."

But I won't. "What if they come while I'm gone?"

So the old man brings mats and blankets from home, and we lie down, in a corner, to sleep.

I have terrible dreams. Dreams of my mother and father flying home to America and me running after the plane, calling, "Wait for me."

The adhan for *Fajr* awakens me. The words echo deep within me. And I say them just like the muezzin. Abdullah says I have a fine voice, low and melodious. I will make a good muezzin one day.

We search the Great Mosque again. And again we don't find my parents.

Talking helps the time go by.

At the end of the day, we curl up again in a corner. "We'll find them, Insha Allah. Don't worry Bilal."

"But what if we don't?" He doesn't hear me.

He says, "We'll go to *Mina.* They must be there, Insha Allah."

If God wills.

So the next day, we walk and we walk, in the blistering heat, with thousands of others, like a river of people. Abdullah says it was the place where Abraham was to sacrifice his son. There's a sea of tents. How will we ever find them?

Abdullah talks to the police in Arabic. They know him and are friendly. They rub my head and smile and nod. Abdullah says they'll keep a lookout for my parents.

We don't find them in Mina. And the day comes when we must go to Arafat, where all the pilgrims will gather.

"They will be there," says Abdullah. "They must. For without Arafat, there is no Hajj."

More than two million people are gathered there. We climb to the top of *Jabal Rahma*, the Mount of Mercy. I am a little angry. Where are they? I lift up my hands like the others, and I pray, "Send my parents!"

After Arafat, even Abdullah looks discouraged. "I was so sure we'd find them there."

"Something has happened to them," I say and wait for Abdullah to deny it.

Finally his face lights up. "Of course. Nothing could have happened. The police would know. They have a list of everyone in the hospitals. Don't worry."

I sigh with relief.

And it's on to *Muzdalifa* and back to Mina, but even when stoning the *Jamrat,* I cannot see them.

Every day that passes makes me more discouraged. I'm afraid to sleep, in case I should miss them, and when I do finally sleep, I have terrible dreams.

They're gone. They're dead. I'm sure they are. But I don't say it out loud, in case it comes true. But I pray, and I pray, and I pray some more. To let them find me, or let me find them. I promise God, I'll never be bad again. I'll do my chores without grumbling. I'll keep my room clean and get my homework done, if only I can find them again.

Only the adhans can please me. For those moments, I can forget.

Hajj is almost done. Only one thing left. The final *tawaf,* so it's back to the Great Mosque we go.

Jabal Rahma: the Mount of Mercy, a small hill in the plain of Arafat. According to legend, it was here that Adam (peace be upon him) and Eve were forgiven for disobeying God.

Muzdalifa: one of the sites of Hajj. Pilgrims stay the night after the day of Arafat.

Jamrat: a stone pillar that represents Satan, the devil. There are three Jamrat found in the plain of Mina, located at the spots where satan appeared to tempt Abraham and Ishmael to disobey God's command of the sacrifice. Abraham and Ishmael picked up a handful of pebbles and tossed them at satan, who ran away. During Hajj, pilgrims repeat this act, tossing seven pebbles at a time at each Jamrat, to symbolize their own rejection of Satan and temptation.

tawaf: the act of going around the Kaaba seven times. Performing it is a part of Hajj.

Zuhr: one of the five daily prayers for Muslims. Zuhr is prayed shortly after midday.

iqaama: the second call to prayer, which signals that prayer is about to begin

Imam: leader of the prayer

Zamzam: a well with a miraculous origin. When Abraham left his wife Hagar and his son Ishmael in the valley of Mecca, it was barren, with no water. When the provision of food and water was finished, baby Ishmael began to cry with thirst, kicking into the sand with his heels. His mother Hagar ran back and forth between the hills Safa and Marwa, in search of water. She ran seven times, and when she came back water had sprung from where Ishmael's feet had been kicking. A miracle, which first quenched baby Ishmael's thirst, today still quenches the thirst of pilgrims from around the world.

We get there in time for *Zuhr.* The hottest time of the day. We hear the muezzin calling us to prayer, and I stop. I stand perfectly still. It's a magical moment for me. And I call the adhan with him. Word for word. Just as well as he can.

Abdullah listens and smiles.

I can't help but say, "I still wish I could give the adhan to all the people in the mosque."

Abdullah's face lights up. "Yes! Why not? I think I can manage it. Not the adhan, but the *iqaama.* Come quickly."

And he leads me through the milling crowds and straight up to the leader of the prayer. And he explains in Arabic and with his hands. And the *Imam* looks at me kindly.

He unfastens the microphone around his neck and puts it around my own. Nervously, I wait for the lines to be formed. I hope I don't forget the words. Or make a mistake. That would be awful.

Abdullah nods. I say, "Mom and Dad, it's me, Bilal. Meet me at *Zamzam* after Zuhr." My voice booms down from speakers on the minarets, echoing across the hills of the ancient city of Mecca. The city of Abraham and of his great-grandson Muhammad, peace be on them. It's a wonderful feeling. I close my eyes and begin:

"Allahu Akbar, Allahu Akbar. " God is Great! God is Great!

"Ashadu an Lailla ha illallah." I declare there is no god but the one God.

"Ashadu anna Muhammadur rasullallah." I declare that Muhammad is His messenger.

"Haya las salah." Come to prayer.

"Haya lal falah." Come to success.

"Qad qaama tis salah. Qad qaama tis salah." Prayer is beginning, Prayer is beginning.

"Allahu Akbar. Allahu Akbar." God is great! God is great!

"La illaha illallah." There is no god but the one God.

68

And then the moment is gone. My dream has come true. But I can't be happy till I see my parents. Till I know they are safe.

And we pray Zuhr, right there, behind the Imam. And I pray and pray, that they will be there, at the well of Zamzam.

And when we're done, we squeeze our way through the crush of people as quickly as the crowds will let us, to Zamzam. And we wait. And wait. The crowds are thick as before. Every colour of people on the earth passing by. Then, suddenly, the crowd parts a little. And two people, a man and a woman, looking confused and hopeful, are coming toward us.

I'm lost in their hugs and smothered with their kisses, while Abdullah watches, a big happy smile on his face.

We're all laughing and crying at the very same time, and Abdullah's eyes are shining. He hugs Dad and nods to my mother. And the stories come tumbling out. And it seems as if everywhere we went, we just missed my parents by a few moments. They were there at Arafat, but with all the crowds and confusion, we couldn't see them.

Over my father's shoulder I can see the hill of Safa, and I hold on a little tighter. Now I know how *Hagar* and *Ishmael* must have felt when Abraham left them here alone.

Abdullah bids us farewell, then picks up his broom and dustpan. "I have work to do." He rubs my head and says, "Remember me in your prayers."

"And you remember us."

He nods and then, even while I'm watching, he melts into the crowd and is gone. I shiver at how easily he disappears.

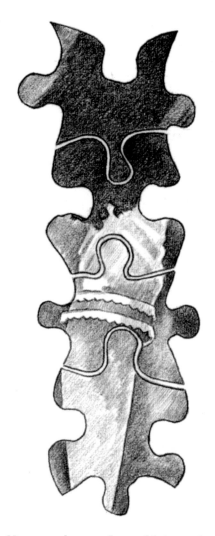

Hagar: the mother of Ishmael and a wife of Prophet Abraham (peace be upon him).

Ishmael: one of the sons of Prophet Abraham (peace be upon him). From Ishmael's (peace be upon him) children and grandchildren came Prophet Muhammad (peace be upon him).

The Hajj

Hajj is the journey of a lifetime, a way of centring Muslims, bringing them from every corner of the globe, back to where it all began—to the city of **Mecca.**

Like electrons circling the nucleus of an atom, we circle the **Kaaba**, the first temple of God, that Abraham and his son Ishmael (peace be upon them) built.

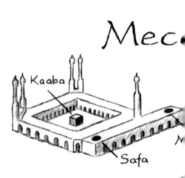

Mec

And like Hagar, mother of Ishmael (peace be upon them), we run back and forth between the hills of **Safa** and **Marwa,** hoping God will answer our need, as He answered hers.

At **Mina,** we gather in a tent city as far as the eye can see, over two million Muslims strong. Then on to the plain of **Arafat.** Is this a dress rehearsal for the Day of Judgment? In pilgrim garb, you can't tell the peasant from the king. All are equal.

And when the sun has set, we leave for **Muzdalifa.** We gather our pebbles and are ready for the next stage.

Back to **Mina** and the stoning of the Jamrat. These are the pillars of stone that represent the devil, who tried to sway Abraham and Ishmael (peace be upon them) from the sacrifice God asked of them. And we cast our pebbles, as did they—but against the pillars. We are rejecting Satan.

And at the end, if the **Hajj** is accepted, we emerge as if newly born, with all past sins obliterated and our slates wiped clean. We are ready to devote the rest of our lives to the service of God.

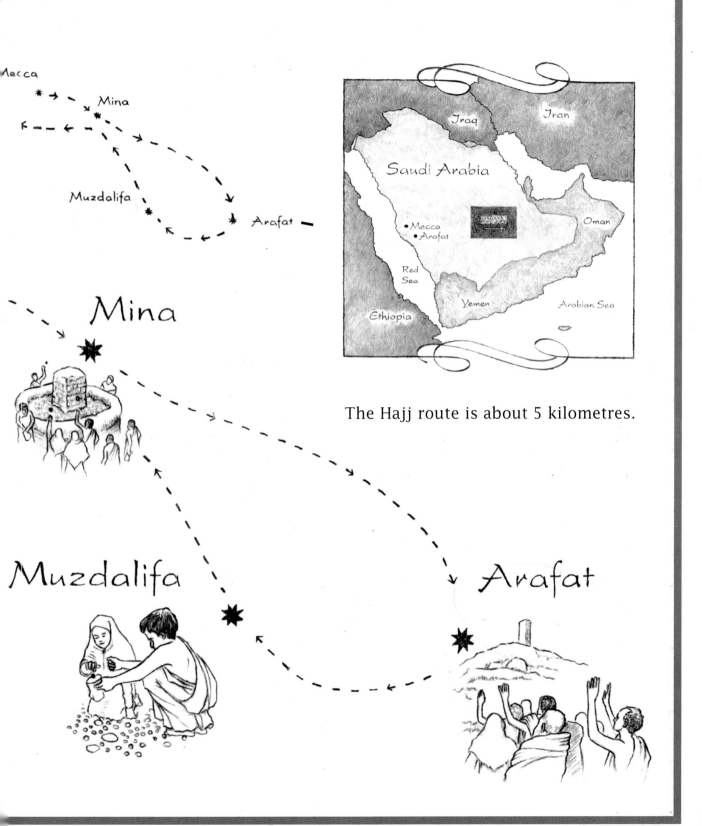

Mecca

Mina

Muzdalifa

Arafat

Saudi Arabia

Iraq

Iran

Oman

Mecca
Arafat

Red
Sea

Yemen

Arabian Sea

Ethiopia

The Hajj route is about 5 kilometres.

Mina

Muzdalifa

Arafat

ONE BIG FAMILY
by Rukhsana Khan

Everyone walking on the face of the earth
Came from one woman and man,
So why should we fight? We should be making peace
And doing all the good that we can.

One big family.
One big family.
Let's live together in harmony.
We're one big family.

Whether we're from the north or south,
From the east or west or in between,
We all know what love is about,
And it hurts when people are mean.

One big family.
One big family.
Let's live together in harmony.
We're one big family.